147

The grand opening was the next day.
"I declare this Sunflower Oil Factory open!"
said Farmer Pickles. And he snipped the ribbon
in half.

"Hooray for Farmer Pickles!" cheered Bob.

"And hooray for Sumsy and Scoop!" said Farmer
Pickles, proudly.

"Ha, ha!" laughed Sumsy. "When we work
together, it's as easy as one, two, three!"

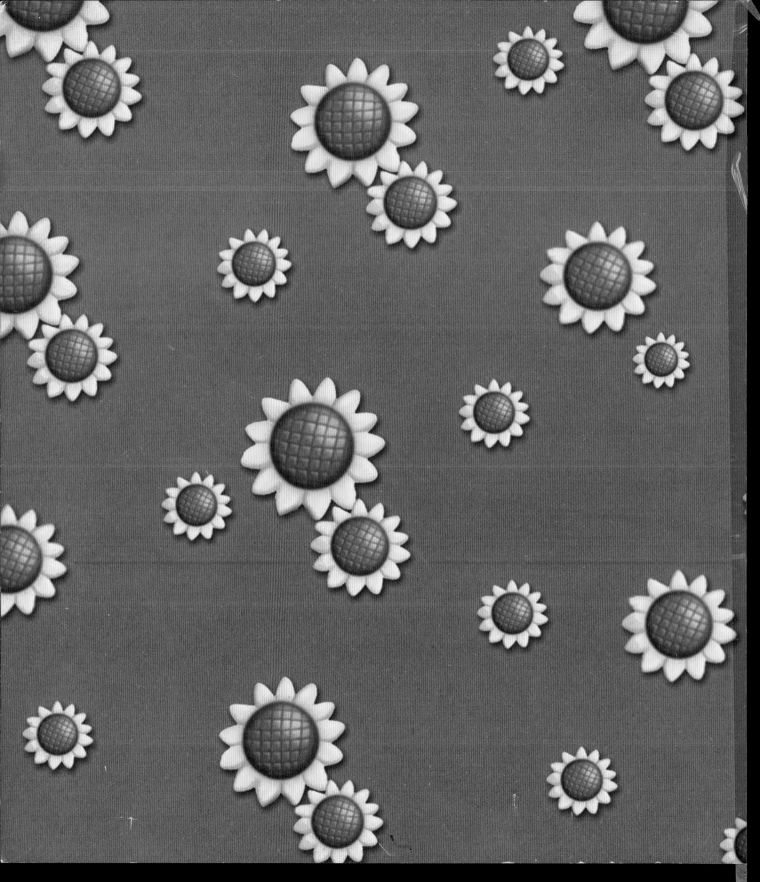

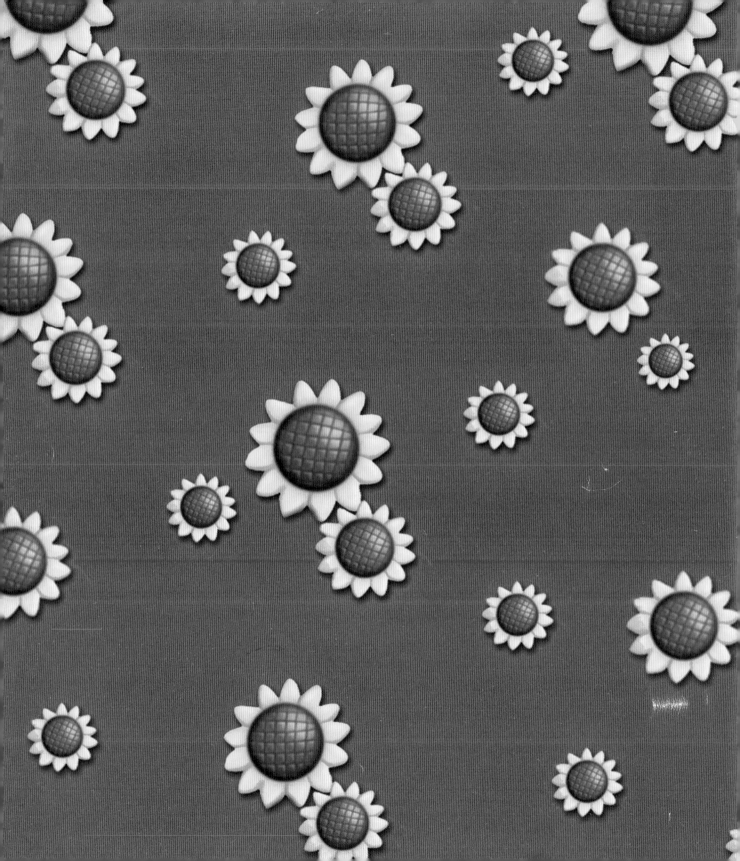

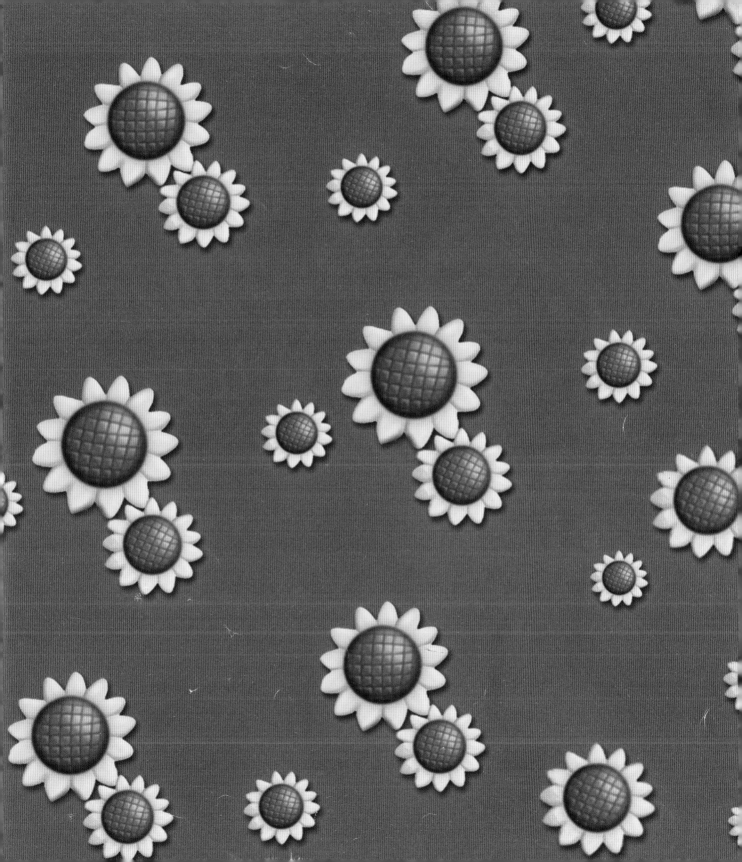

Bob's Favourite Tales

EGMONT

We bring stories to life

This edition published in Great Britain 2011 by Egmont UK Limited
239 Kensington High Street, London W8 6SA

Endpapers and illustrations by Craig Cameron and Puisar.

Based on the television series Bob the Builder
© 2011 HIT Entertainment and Keith Chapman.

ISBN 978 1 4052 6175 3

50932/1

Printed in Italy

Contents

Bob and the Big Plan

Bob and the team were busy at work, building a bigger office for Mr Adams the architect.

"I'll need more space if I win the competition to plan a new town in Sunflower Valley," Mr Adams explained. "I've been working on my model for weeks!"

"We used to go to Sunflower Valley on holiday when I was young!" said Bob.

But Bob felt sad when he saw the model.
Mr Adams had turned Sunflower Valley
into a noisy city, packed with busy roads
and big buildings.

"I'm taking this to the town hall, so everyone
can have a good look," said Mr Adams.
"The judging is the day after tomorrow.
Goodbye, Bob!"

"**W**hy don't you enter the competition, Bob?" asked Muck, later on.

"Great idea!" said Dizzy.

"Ho, ho! I'm a builder, not an architect like Mr Adams," said Bob. "And I have lots of work to do here."

Dizzy and Muck were disappointed. But the next morning, Bob changed his mind. He didn't want Sunflower Valley to be spoiled.

"**W**hat about the job here, Bob?" asked Scoop, sounding worried.

"Can you finish the foundations by yourselves?" said Bob. "The competition is tomorrow!"

"Can we build it?" said Scoop.

"Yes, we can!" chimed Roley and Muck.

"Er, yeah, I think so," added Lofty.

Back at the yard, Bob was looking through his books for ideas.

"Wow! Look at these buildings, Pilchard," said Bob. "I'll need a Big Plan to win this competition!"

"Miaow!" said Pilchard.

Later, Roley and Bird were watching Bob sketch his ideas for Sunflower Valley. But when Bob drew houses, they didn't look right.

"Toot, toot!" squawked Bird. He was showing Bob his nest.

"Good idea, Bird!" smiled Bob. "I'll have houses that don't spoil the countryside, like yours!"

"Brilliant!" said Roley.

Bob had almost finished his model,
when he heard a noise outside.
Vrrooom! Vrrooom!

Just then, Mr Bentley appeared on a shiny
off-road vehicle. "Hello, Bob," he said. "I'm just
taking Scrambler to the town hall – he's part of
the prize for the competition!"

"Nice to meet you, Scrambler!" smiled Bob.

19

At Mr Adams' office, the team was in trouble. Dizzy was pouring out cement for the foundations, when Scoop noticed the markers were in the wrong place. Concrete spilled everywhere!

"Oh, no! What are we going to do?" worried Scoop.

"We'll have to fetch Bob before the concrete goes hard!" said Muck.

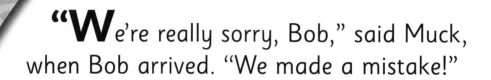

"We're really sorry, Bob," said Muck, when Bob arrived. "We made a mistake!"

"Now you won't have time to finish your model," sighed Dizzy.

"If we work quickly, we can move the concrete before it sets and use it later," said Bob, kindly.

"Reduce, reuse, recycle!" said the team. And they worked together until the job was done.

Bob had just arrived back in the yard when, suddenly, the lights went out.

"It's a power cut!" said Bob. "Fetch some lamps, Muck."

While Bob finished his model, he told the machines about the different ways to make power. "We'll use the sun and the wind to power Sunflower Valley!" he said.

"Wind turbines and solar panels! How cool!" said Scoop, excitedly.

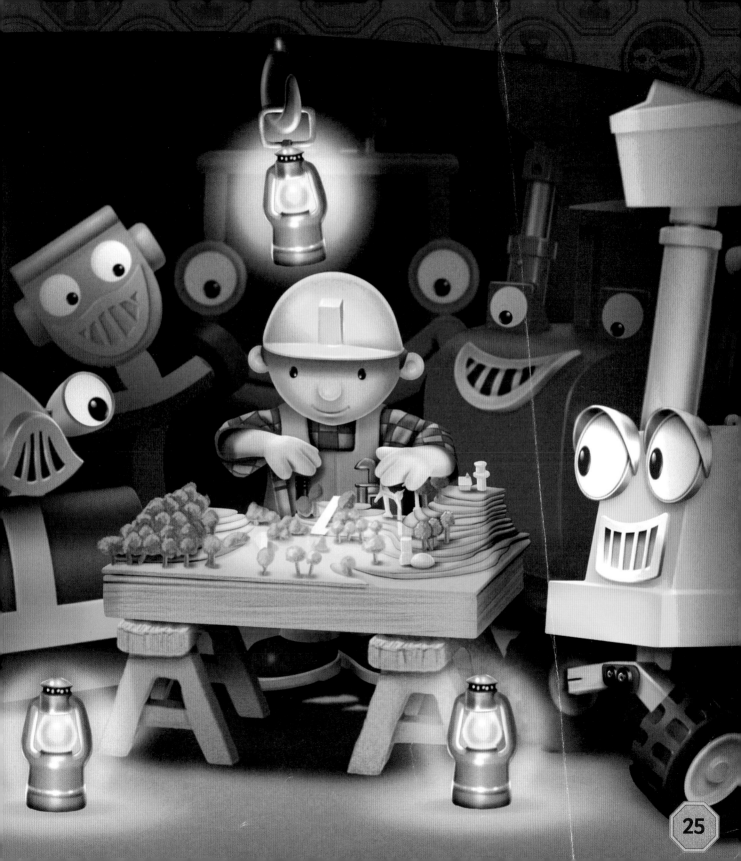

The next day at the town hall, Mr Adams was finishing his speech when Bob appeared.

"Wait!" shouted Bob. "Here's my Big Plan for Sunflower Valley! We'd use recycled things to build a beautiful town," he explained. "Everything would be powered by water, wind and sun to save energy!"

"Ooh!" and **"Wow!"** went the crowd, when they saw Bob's model.

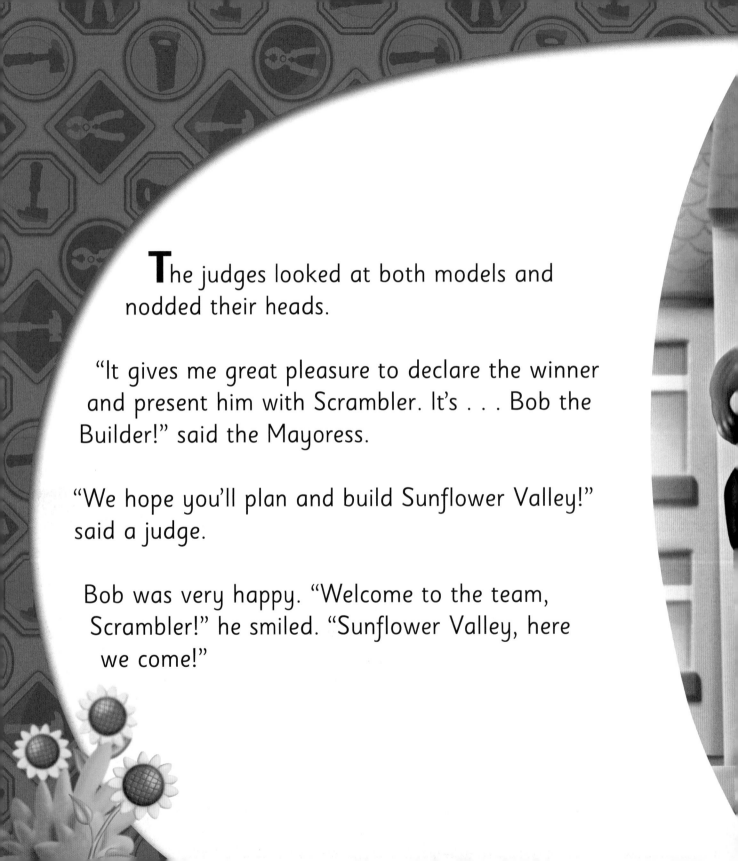

The judges looked at both models and nodded their heads.

"It gives me great pleasure to declare the winner and present him with Scrambler. It's . . . Bob the Builder!" said the Mayoress.

"We hope you'll plan and build Sunflower Valley!" said a judge.

Bob was very happy. "Welcome to the team, Scrambler!" he smiled. "Sunflower Valley, here we come!"

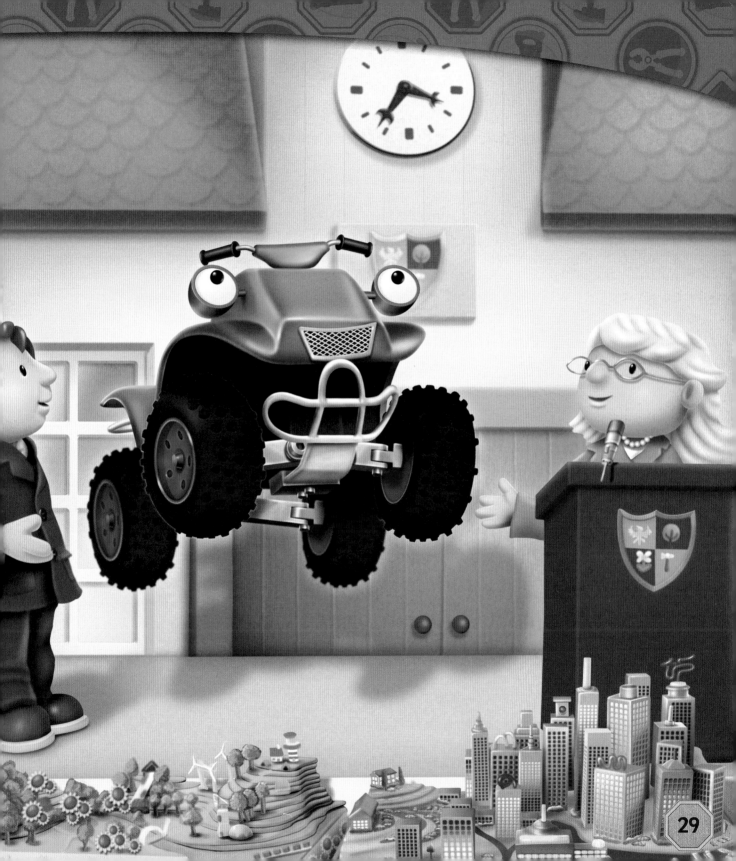

Dizzy and the Talkie-Talkie

One sunny morning, Bob and the team were gathered around a large metal tank in the new yard in Sunflower Valley.

"This will be our new water tank," Bob told the machines. "We can use it to store our water. We will pump the water from the ground through the pipes using a hand pump."

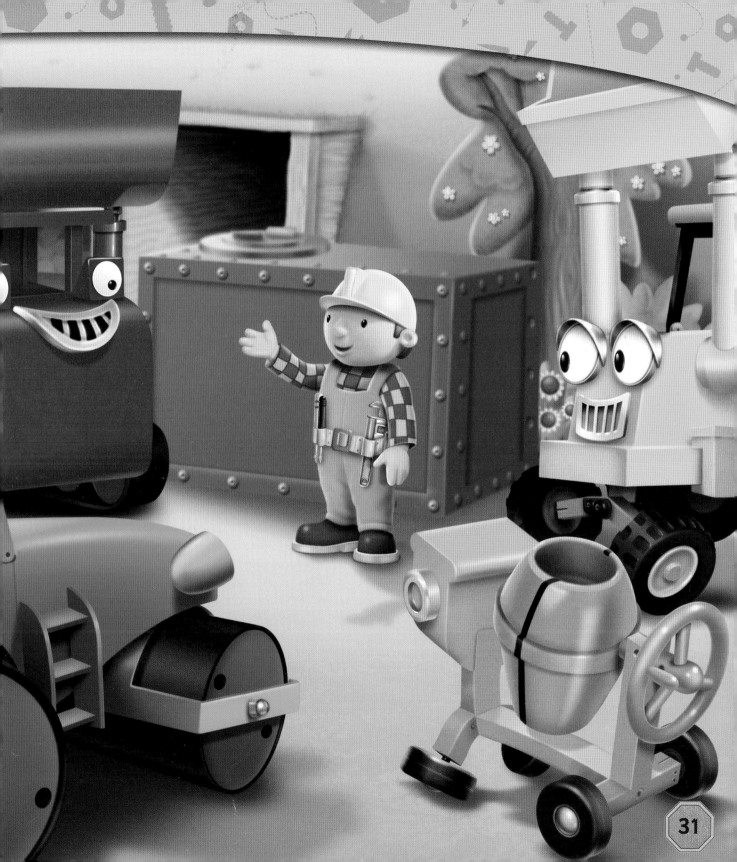

"Hello, everyone!" called Wendy, driving into the yard on Scrambler.

"I've got a present for each of you. They're called talkie-talkies! You can use the headsets to talk to each other wherever you are in Sunflower Valley!" said Wendy, as she handed out the headsets.

"Rock and roll!" smiled Roley.

"That reminds me," said Bob. "We still need some rocks for the tank."

"Dizzy and I can go and find rocks," suggested Scrambler. "We can use the talkie-talkies to let Muck know when we find some. Let's scram!"

"Remember your way so you can get back," called Wendy, as they left.

"**O**K, team? Can we build it?" Bob asked. "Yes, we can!" everyone cheered.

"Then let's get started! Lofty, you will be getting soil out using this special drill so we can reach the water."

"OK, Bob," said Lofty, and he got to work.

"**D**izzy to Scrambler! Can you hear me?" asked Dizzy.

The friends were having fun using the talkie-talkies!

"Cor, look at that big boulder," said Scrambler. "We won't forget we passed that!"

Dizzy and Scrambler came to a sudden stop. There had been a landslide and the path was blocked with rocks!

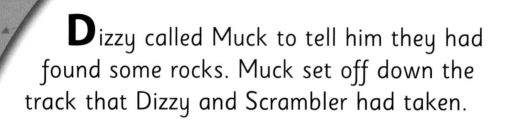

Dizzy called Muck to tell him they had found some rocks. Muck set off down the track that Dizzy and Scrambler had taken.

Very soon, Muck came to the big boulder. "Muck to Dizzy, which way do I go at the big boulder, please?" he asked, using his talkie-talkie.

"Erm, you turn left," Dizzy told Muck.

Muck carried on until he came to two trees that looked like an arch. Dizzy couldn't remember seeing an arch. "Go right, I think," said Dizzy.

"And where do I go at the woods?" asked Muck.

"Erm, I don't remember any woods," replied Dizzy. "Oh, no!" cried Muck. "I'm lost!"

Dizzy had an idea. "What can you see around you?" she asked Muck.

"Erm, a big hill with a cloud on top," replied Muck.

"Cool as a mule, Muck! Coz I see the big hill with the cloud, too," added Scrambler, over his talkie-talkie. "Head for the hill and you should find us."

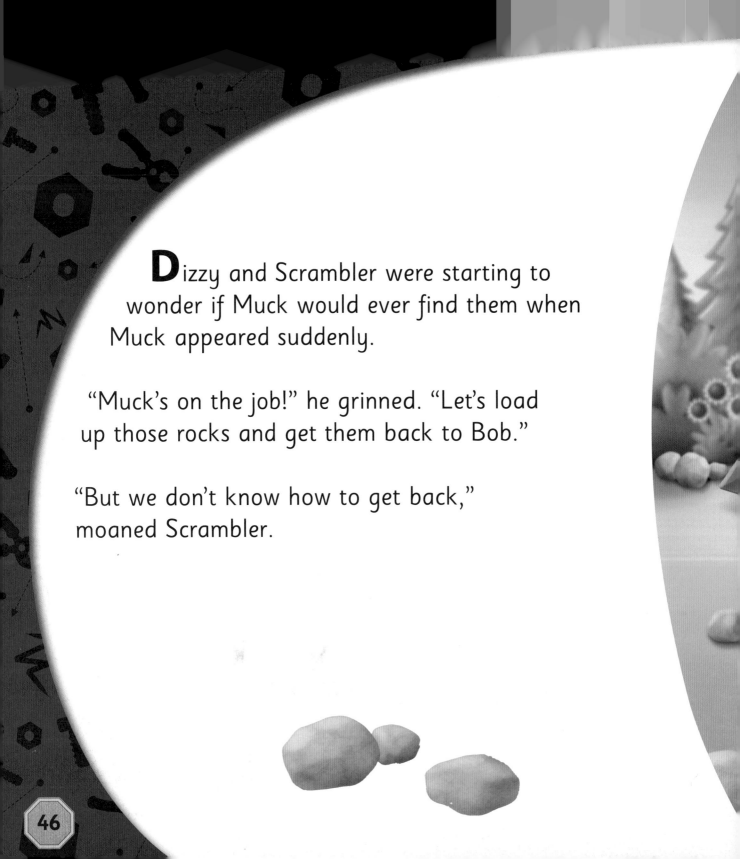

Dizzy and Scrambler were starting to wonder if Muck would ever find them when Muck appeared suddenly.

"Muck's on the job!" he grinned. "Let's load up those rocks and get them back to Bob."

"But we don't know how to get back," moaned Scrambler.

Dizzy remembered how Muck had found them.

"Dizzy to Roley," she whispered into the talkie-talkie. "What big things can you see?"

"A really tall tree, taller than all the others," Roley whispered back.

"Come on!" Dizzy told Roley and Muck. "Let's head for the really tall tree!"

Back at the yard, Bob was beginning to wonder where Dizzy, Scrambler and Muck had got to.

"Call them on the talkie-talkie base unit!" suggested Wendy.

"Bob to Dizzy!" Bob began.

"Dizzy to Bob!" came a voice right behind him. "We're back! And we've got rocks."

Soon the water tank was finished. Wendy tried the pump and the pipes began to rattle.

Splash! Water flew out of the pipes and soaked poor Bob!

"Dizzy to Bob," giggled Dizzy. "Hee, hee, you left the tap on!"

"Oh, Dizzy!" said Bob. And everybody began to laugh! It was another job well done for Bob and the machine team.

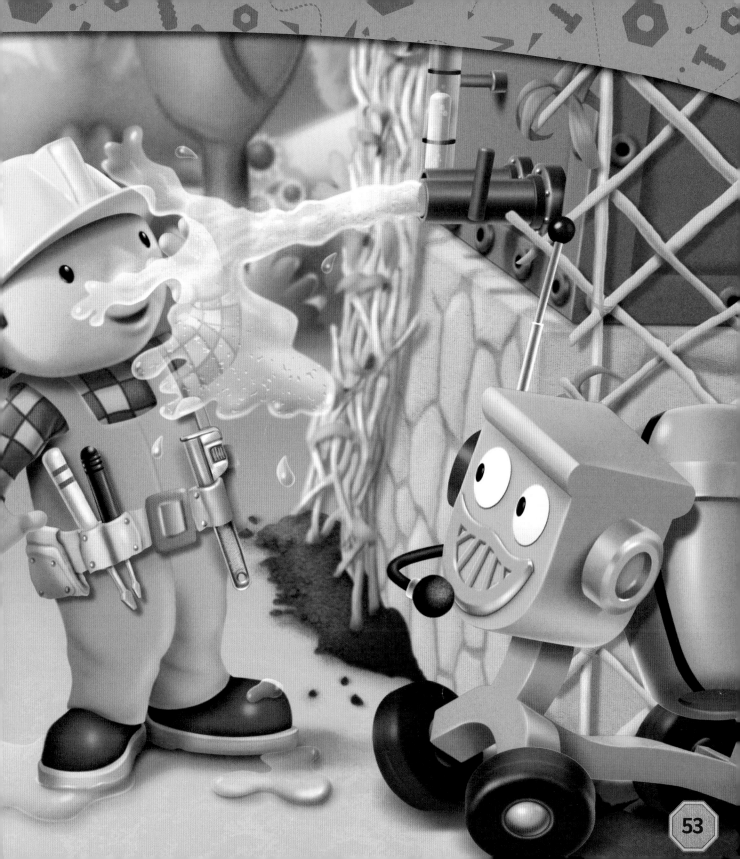

Scrambler and the Off-Road Race

It was a lovely day in Sunflower Valley, and the team had a new job.

"We're building a barn for Farmer Pickles!" announced Bob.

Scruffty was excited. **"Ruff! Ruff!"** he barked, as he raced around Bob's legs.

But Bob didn't have time to play.

Scrambler was excited, too. He really wanted to help Bob and Wendy.

"What will I be doing?" he asked.

Bob shook his head.

"I'm sorry, Scrambler," he said. "But there isn't really a job for you to do."

Scrambler was disappointed. But then Bob had an idea.

"There is something you can do," smiled Bob. "You can take Scruffty for a walk!"

"But that's not a proper job," said Scrambler, sadly.

"Yes it is," replied Bob. "You'll be keeping Scruffty safe."

The whole team was excited about building the barn.

"Can we build it?" Scoop asked.

"Yes, we can!" the machines all cried.

"Er, yeah, I think so," added Lofty.

But poor Scrambler said nothing. He trailed sadly off to walk Scruffty.

Scruffty ran on ahead, panting excitedly.

"Ruff! Ruff!"

Scrambler followed slowly. He felt miserable.

"I can't believe I'm walking a dog!" he grumbled. "I thought I was going to get something important to do."

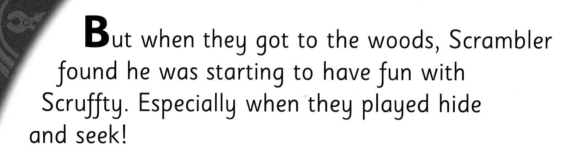

But when they got to the woods, Scrambler found he was starting to have fun with Scruffty. Especially when they played hide and seek!

When it was Scruffty's turn to hide, he ran off instead. The little dog didn't understand how to play the game!

Back at the site, everyone was working very hard.

Lofty was helping Bob and Wendy set up a wooden frame for the walls and roof of the barn.

Dizzy was pouring concrete to make the floor, and Roley was rolling it flat.

Scrambler and Scruffty chased each other until they found themselves in a beautiful valley, full of twisty paths and ditches.

"Wow!" exclaimed Scrambler. "Let's have an off-road race!"

"Ruff!" barked Scruffty, running ahead. The race was on!

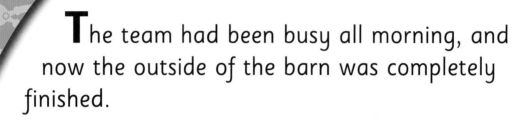

The team had been busy all morning, and now the outside of the barn was completely finished.

"Excellent!" said Bob. "Now we need to build some shelves for Farmer Pickles to store things on."

"We'll need to concentrate," said Wendy. "It's a good thing Scruffty's not here!"

Scrambler and Scruffty were having the best time ever. They raced over rocks and through streams, getting very mucky.

"RUFF! RUFF! RUFF!" barked Scruffty, running through a hollow log.

"WHEEEEE!" cried Scrambler. "You can't catch me!"

At last, Scruffty landed in a big muddy puddle. **Splash!**

Back at the barn, work was finished. Bob and Wendy were having a rest and a cup of tea.

"I wonder where Scrambler's got to with Scruffty?" wondered Wendy, looking around.

Just then, Scrambler rumbled up. He was carrying something in his trailer.

"**S**cruffty's asleep!" said Scrambler.
"But I'm not tired." He tried not to yawn.

"See . . . dog-walking is a proper job," said Bob,
lifting Scruffty from the trailer. "And you made
a friend!"

Scruffty woke up and licked his new friend's
nose. **"Ruff!"**

"Making friends is wicked!" Scrambler
grinned happily.

Wendy and the Surprise Party

In Sunflower Valley, Bob and the team were building a dome.

"You've done a great job getting all the parts, Wendy," said Bob. "So I think you should be in charge."

"Oh Bob, I'd love to!" replied Wendy. But then she began to look worried.

As Bob walked away, Wendy whispered to the machines:

"I need you to help me keep Bob busy. I'm planning a surprise party for him tomorrow night at the dome! Mr Bentley is letting everyone know."

"But the dome isn't built yet!" cried Muck.

Wendy wasn't worried about building the dome. But she was worried about how she was going to organise the party! Bob and the machines were ready to start.

"Can we build it?" asked Scoop.

"Yes, we can!" replied the machines.

"Er . . . yeah, I think so," added Lofty.

They dug the foundations and made a timber frame.

Then Scrambler whizzed in with Mr and Mrs Bentley.

"Hello, everybody!" said Mr Bentley. "We are here to pick a spot for our new house!"

"We're going to live in a tent while we build it," added Mrs Bentley.

"I'll show you where to pitch it," offered Wendy. But she was really leaving so she could organise the party!

Wendy had just picked up her phone when Scoop arrived.

"Can you come back and tell Bob what to do next?" asked Scoop.

"Bernard will help you with the party tonight," said Mrs Bentley.

"Tonight?" replied Wendy. "But the party is tomorrow!"

Mr Bentley had told everyone to come on the wrong night! Wendy decided that she would organise the party when she got back from the building site.

"We've got to be quick or it won't be finished in time," said Wendy, when she saw Bob and Dizzy stood looking at the dome pieces.

"In time for what?" asked Bob.

"Oh, nothing Bob!" replied Wendy, hurriedly.

Soon the first layer of the dome was complete. Wendy decided to sneak away to make the phone calls about the party.

"Wendy, what do we need to do next?" asked Bob.

"Just look at my notes," called Wendy. "It's all in there!" And then she zoomed away on Muck, leaving Bob looking confused.

Wendy arrived at her mobile home and found the Bentleys there.

"I'm just calling Mrs Percival," said Mr Bentley.

"Oh, I'll talk to her," said Wendy, nervously.

Just then, Farmer Pickles arrived with everyone from Bobsville, including Mrs Percival! Wendy was worried that Bob might see them.

But Wendy and Muck had to go back to the site.

"You get back to the dome and we'll sort out everything for the party," said Mr Bentley.

"Oh no, I can deal with it," said Wendy. "Don't do anything, Mr Bentley. I will be back soon."

At the site, Wendy soon saw that Bob hadn't left space for the doors into the dome!

"**Oops**, I'll just have to start this layer again!" said Bob.

"But that will take too long!" said Wendy.

"Wendy, why don't you let Mr Bentley organise the party?" whispered Muck. "You can't organise the dome and the party at the same time."

Just then, Scrambler zoomed in with Mr Bentley.

"Oh, Mr Bentley, I'm sorry I wouldn't let you help," said Wendy, looking at Muck. "Can you organise the party?"

"I would be delighted!" replied Mr Bentley, and Scrambler zoomed off!

With the team working together, the dome was soon finished. Bob went to his mobile home to get some cordial to celebrate.

But when he returned, the dome was decorated with balloons and everyone was wearing party hats!

"Surprise!" cried the Bobsvillagers.

"I don't believe it!" said Bob. "Wendy, when did you manage to organise all this?"

"I've had lots of help!" smiled Wendy.

And then everyone cheered, "Hooray for Sunflower Valley!" as fireworks exploded.

Roley and the Woodland Walk

It was a very hot day in Sunflower Valley.

Bob and Wendy were on their way to build workbenches and fit big tools in the workshop.

"We don't need any help, today," said Bob. "So you can all have the day off!"

The machines wanted to keep cool in the shade. So off they all went to the shelter to play 'I Spy'. Except for Roley ...

Roley set off into Sunflower Valley to look for his friend, Birdie.

"Birdie," called Roley. "It's your friend, Roley. Birdie! Where are you?"

Roley came to a pond in the clearing, but the hot weather had dried up all the water. Next to the pond, he saw Birdie, looking sad. Roley didn't know what was wrong.

"**Y**ou're not whistling," worried Roley. "Are you too hot?"

Birdie chirped weakly. Roley wondered how he could help. "Maybe I could find you somewhere to keep cool?"

Just then, Birdie's chicks flew on to Roley's cab. As Roley set off to find some shade, a squirrel hopped out of the trees. He was hot, too. "Don't worry," said Roley, kindly. "I'll come back for you."

Roley gave Birdie and her chicks a ride to the storeroom. When they arrived, they flew off his cab and headed for the workshop.

"No, no! Not in there. That's where Bob and Wendy are working," he said, and guided them into the cool storeroom.

Then Roley set off to fetch the squirrel.

Wendy and Bob were building a new cupboard to keep all the tools tidy.

They went to the storeroom to get the first big tool – the saw.

They didn't see Birdie and her chicks nestling under the cover!

Roley zoomed back to the clearing. "It's all right, little squirrel," said Roley. "I've got a lovely place for you out of the sun."

Suddenly, three more squirrels scampered down the trees. "Climb aboard," smiled Roley. Just as he was about to leave, a family of otters dashed out of the bushes. They were hot and thirsty, too.

"Stay here. I'll be right back!" said Roley.

Roley dropped the squirrels off at the storeroom, and then went to fetch the otters.

With the tool cupboard finished, Wendy and Bob wanted to fit the big saw. But when Wendy found the instructions, they were full of holes!

"Oh, no! We can't read this," said Wendy. "Something's been pecking at them!"

Bob and Wendy couldn't fit the saw without the instructions. They decided to fit the next big tool instead – the drill.

As Wendy pulled off the cover, the squirrels scurried away to hide.

"Look, Wendy!" cried Bob. "These instructions are torn, too."

They were really puzzled now!

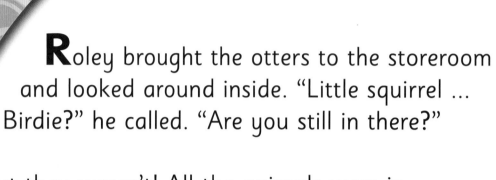

Roley brought the otters to the storeroom and looked around inside. "Little squirrel ... Birdie?" he called. "Are you still in there?"

But they weren't! All the animals were in the workshop.

Roley didn't want Bob to see the animals, so he thought of a plan. "I found Birdie. Um ... she's not well. She needs our help!" he said, making it up.

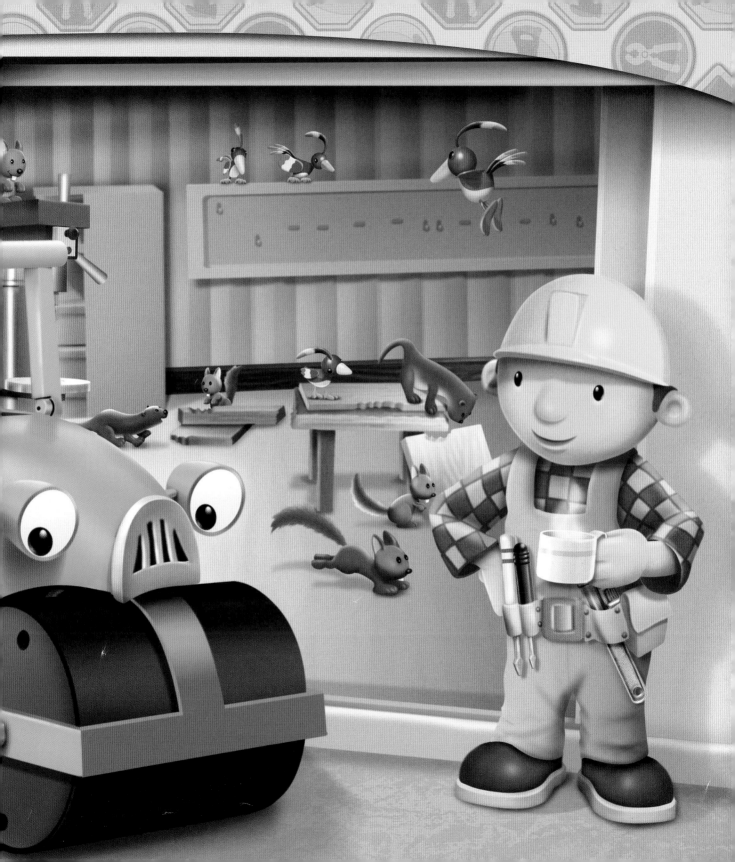

Roley took Bob to the dried-up pond.

"Birdie must be thirsty!" said Bob. "When ponds dry up, birds and animals can't get any water. The best way to help is to put some out for them." Then Bob poured water from his flask. "Now when Birdie comes back, she can have a drink."

Then, Bob and Roley rolled back to the workshop.

Back at the workshop, Wendy had some news for them. "Bob!" she called. "I know why everything was chewed and pecked! The workshop was full of animals! I gave them some water and they've all gone away happy."

Roley felt bad, so he told Bob what had happened. "Don't worry, Roley," said Bob. "You were only trying to help."

Suddenly, Roley had a brilliant idea ...

Roley asked the other machines to help gather up old bits of wood so Bob and Wendy could build a bird table. That way, his woodland friends would have food and water, and he would see them all the time.

The team worked together and soon the bird table was finished. "Rock and roll!" smiled Roley.

And now, whenever the animals get thirsty or hot, they visit Roley's bird table.

Sumsy and the Sunflower Spill

Farmer Pickles was getting ready for the grand opening of his new Sunflower Oil Factory.

"There's just one more job to do," he said. "I need somewhere for all these boxes."

"No problem," smiled Bob. "We'll build you a bottle depot."

"Thanks, Bob," said Farmer Pickles. "Now I've got a surprise for you! Meet ..."

"**S**umsy the forklift! She's going to move the boxes with the bottles of sunflower oil from the factory to the storage depot."

"I can pack 'em! I can stack 'em!" smiled Sumsy. "Hi, everyone!"

"Hello, Sumsy," said Bob, Scoop and Travis.

She looked at Travis. "One, two, three boxes. I love counting!" Sumsy laughed.

"**R**ight!" said Bob. "I'd better get started building this depot." And off he went.

Farmer Pickles and Travis went too, and Scoop and Sumsy were left on their own.

"I'm Scoop!" said Scoop. "I know everything about Sunflower Valley. I'll show you around. Follow me!"

"What about the boxes?" Sumsy worried. But Scoop had rolled away.

The first stop on Scoop's tour was the homestead. Then he showed Sumsy the workshops and the storerooms. "We've plenty of time to work," said Scoop.

But Sumsy looked sad. She knew there were lots of boxes to be moved.

Soon, they reached the site where Bob and the team were building the bottle depot.

"**H**i, Scoop!" smiled Dizzy.

"Hi, everyone," called Scoop. "This is Sumsy!
Sumsy, meet Dizzy, Muck and ... Roley."

"Rock and ro-ho-ole!" said Roley.

"Three machines. Three!" counted Sumsy.
"Three boxes is how many I can fit on my forklift.
I can pack 'em, I can stack 'em!" she laughed, and
raced away.

Just then, Farmer Pickles arrived with a big crate. "Look what I've got here!" he said. "A bottle-labelling machine."

He pressed a button and labels began to fly out, sticking themselves to Dizzy, Roley and Bob!

"We're not bottles! Ha, ha!" smiled Dizzy.

"What a sticky situation!" said Farmer Pickles. "I hope Sumsy brings those boxes of bottles soon."

Inside the factory, Sumsy was hard at work. "Coming through! Ten bottles in every box," she said, whizzing past Scoop.

"Wait!" moaned Scoop. "I haven't shown you all the factory yet! How can I tell you things if you keep driving off?"

Sumsy raced away, with Scoop chasing behind.

Scoop caught up with Sumsy and swerved in front of her to make her stop.

Sumsy screeched to a halt, but it was too late. **CRASH!** The boxes flew off her forklift and smashed on the ground.

"Oh, no!" cried Scoop.

Sumsy and Scoop went to look at the mess. The bottles were broken and oil had spilled everywhere.

Meanwhile, Bob and the team had nearly finished building the bottle depot.

"Well done, team. We're almost ready for your bottles, Farmer Pickles," he said.

"But then we need labels on the bottles," worried Farmer Pickles. "Where's Sumsy?"

"Here she comes!" said Dizzy, as Sumsy trundled sadly towards them.

Farmer Pickles saw the boxes of broken bottles. "Oh dear!" he gasped.

"I'm sorry, Farmer Pickles," said Sumsy. "I was trying to do my job, when, erm …"

"It was me," said Scoop. "I got in Sumsy's way. I was showing her around the valley."

When Scoop found out that the bottles all needed labels, he felt very sorry. "There's not enough time!" he cried.

"Three boxes fit on my forklift, and two fit in your digger," Sumsy said to Scoop, kindly. "We'll work together to get the job done quicker!"

So that's what they did. Before long, all the boxes were safely in the depot and all the bottles had labels.

Bob finished building the depot wall and the factory was ready to open, just in time!

The grand opening was the next day. "I declare this Sunflower Oil Factory open!" said Farmer Pickles. And he snipped the ribbon in half.

"Hooray for Farmer Pickles!" cheered Bob.

"And hooray for Sumsy and Scoop!" said Farmer Pickles, proudly.

"Ha, ha!" laughed Sumsy. "When we work together, it's as easy as one, two, three!"

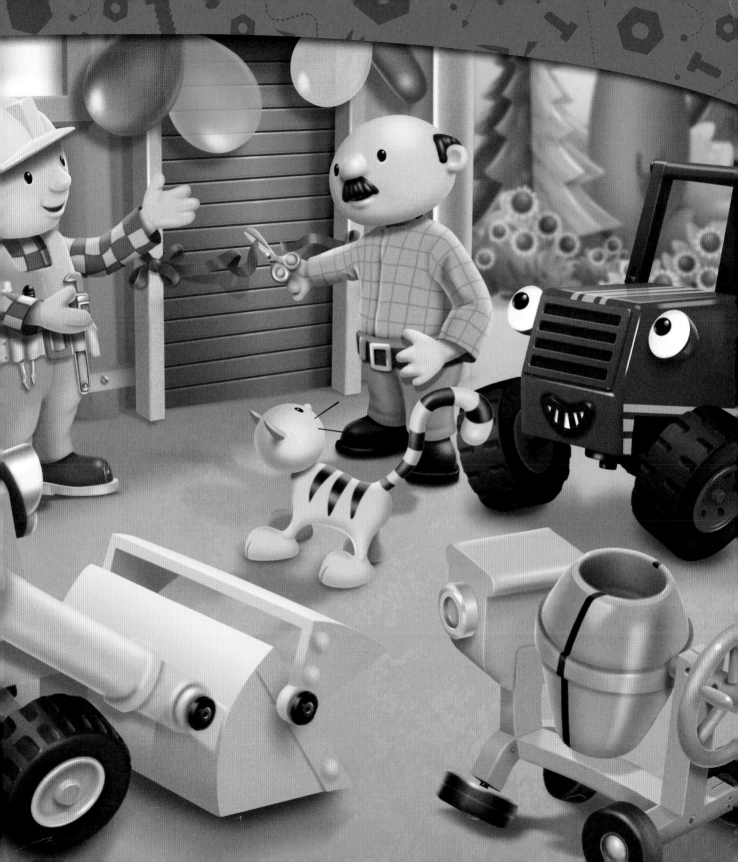

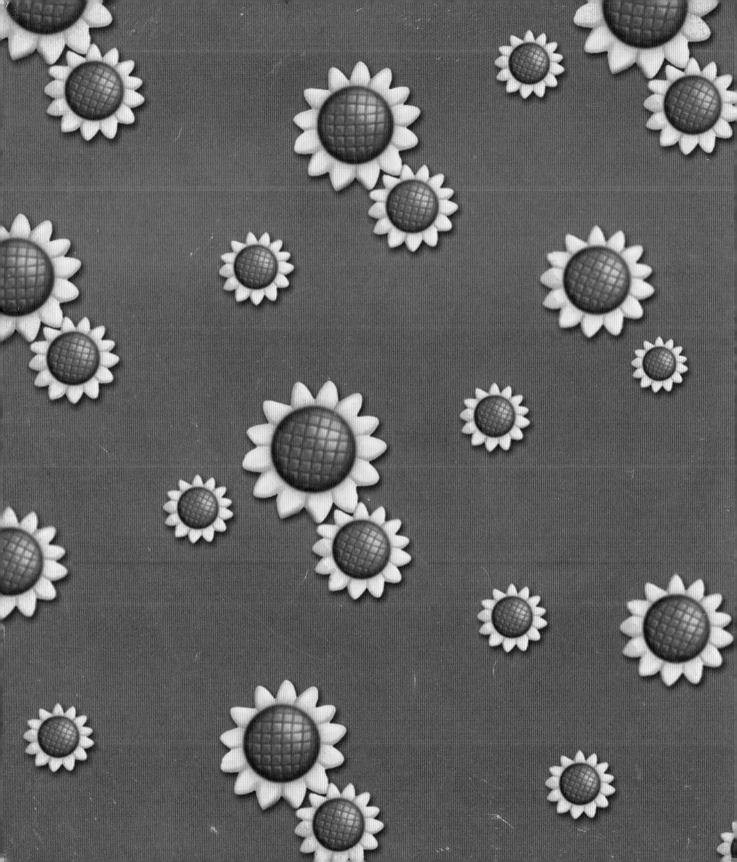